Aisha the Princess and the Pea Fairy

Special thanks to Tracey West

ISBN 978-0-545-85199-2

10 9 8 7 6 5 4 3 2 1   16 17 18 19 20

Printed in the U.S.A.   40

First edition, January 2016

Aisha the Princess and the Pea Fairy

By Daisy Meadows

SCHOLASTIC INC.

The Fairyland Palace
Fairy Tale Lane
Rachel's House
Tippington Town

Jack Frost's
Ice Castle
Forest
Tiptop Castle

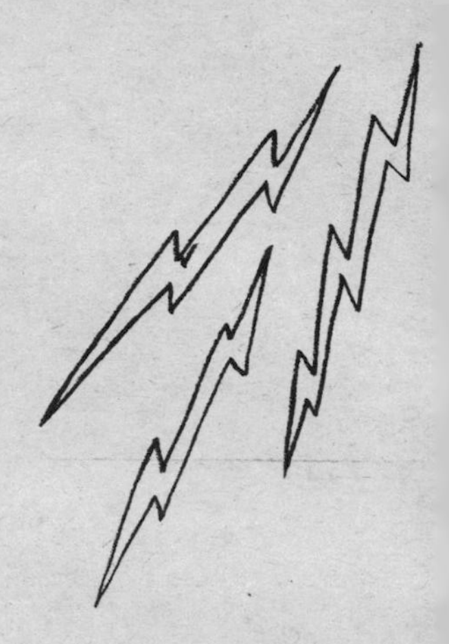

The Fairy Tale Fairies are in for a shock!
Cinderella won't run at the strike of the clock.
No one can stop me—I've plotted and planned,
And I'll be the fairest one in all of the land.

It will take someone handsome and witty and clever
To stop storybook endings forever and ever.
But to see fairies suffer great trouble and strife,
Will make me live happily all of my life!

Contents

A Rainy Morning

"Rain, rain, go away," Kirsty Tate sang gloomily.

Her best friend, Rachel Walker, joined in. *"Come again some other day."*

The two girls were looking out the window of their bedroom in Tiptop Castle. They had arrived a few days before for the Fairy Tale Festival. Each day, the festival organizers had planned a special fairy tale–themed activity for the guests. Today they were supposed to go on a fairy tale walk through the woods.

"No walk through the woods today," Kirsty said as she pushed a lock of brown hair away from her face. Outside, a steady rain fell on the grounds of Tiptop Castle. Puddles formed on the green lawn and water splashed up from the castle moat. The sky was as gray as the smooth castle stones.

"Amy said they were going to come up with a special activity for us," Rachel said. "It might be a movie. That will be fun."

"I know," Kirsty said. "I guess I just don't like rain. It makes me feel . . . blah. And until the activity starts, there's nothing to do."

Rachel looked thoughtful. "Maybe it's good that we have some free time. There are still two of the Fairy Tale Fairies' missing items to find!"

"Of course! Why didn't I think of that?" Kirsty wondered. "Come on, let's look in the book."

Rachel and Kirsty were both friends of the fairies. On their first day at Tiptop

Castle, Hannah the Happily Ever After Fairy had come to see them. She had invited them to visit Fairy Tale Lane, home of the seven Fairy Tale Fairies. Each of the fairies had a magic object that helped them take care of a different fairy tale.

But Jack Frost, that troublemaker, had stolen all seven magic objects. He wanted to be the star of every fairy tale! While Jack Frost had the objects, the fairy tale characters were lost and couldn't get back to their stories. The pages in *The Fairies' Book of Fairy Tales* had all gone blank.

Rachel picked up the book from the dressing table and leafed through it. "So far, we've found five of the objects," she said. "And five fairy tales are back in the book."

"*Sleeping Beauty*, *Snow White*, *Cinderella*, *The Frog Princess*, and *Beauty and the Beast*," said Kirsty. "So which fairy tales are left?"

"*The Princess and the Pea* and *The Little Mermaid*," Rachel replied.

"Hmm," Kirsty said. "I haven't read either of those stories in a while."

"Well, we could see if we can find them in the castle library," Rachel suggested. "Maybe we can find clues that could tell us what Jack Frost is up to next."

"Good idea," Kirsty agreed, and the two girls headed to the grand castle staircase.

The big chandelier glittered overhead as they walked downstairs.

"*The Princess and the Pea*," Kirsty mused. "That's the one where a lost girl shows up at a castle on a rainy night, right? She says she's a princess, but the queen doesn't believe her."

Rachel nodded. "Right. So the queen tests her. She makes her sleep on a tall stack of mattresses and puts a pea on the very bottom. If the girl can feel the pea, it will mean she is a true princess."

"That's kind of silly," Kirsty said. "How could anyone feel a tiny pea under all those mattresses?"

"Well, in the story, it's because the princess has such delicate skin," Rachel explained. "At least I think so. I hope we can find the book in the library."

When the girls reached the main hall, they found a surprising sight waiting for them. Many of the Fairy Tale Festival guests and organizers were running around and looking confused.

Kirsty stopped Omri, one of the other children the girls had made friends with.

"What's going on?" Kirsty asked him.

"It's so weird!" Omri replied. "When I got back to my room after breakfast, my mattress was missing!"

"You mean your whole bed was gone?" Rachel asked.

Omri shook his head. "No, just the mattress. And then when I went to tell one of the organizers, a bunch of kids were saying they were missing their mattresses, too."

"Maybe someone took them to be cleaned," Rachel guessed.

"That's what Amy thought, but none of the other organizers knew about it," Omri explained. "Like I said, it's weird."

A girl ran down the stairs. "My mattress is missing!"

"So is mine!" shouted a boy.

An organizer dressed like a fairy tale prince held up his hands. "Calm down, everyone! We'll figure this out."

Rachel pulled Kirsty aside. "This is very strange. Why would someone be stealing mattresses? And where would they hide them?"

Kirsty's eyes got wide. "Hey, we were just talking about mattresses. In the fairy tale. Maybe—"

Just then, there was a loud knock on the front door of the castle.

"Should we answer it?" Rachel wondered. All of the festival organizers were off looking for the missing mattresses.

"I guess we should," Kirsty replied, and the two girls walked to the big front doors and opened them.

A young woman stood in the rain. Her gray dress was dirty and soaked. Water dripped from her long, dark hair.

"I . . . I think I'm lost," she said. "May I please come in and stay warm and dry?"

Rachel whispered to Kirsty, "I don't know if we are allowed to let strangers into the castle."

"But she looks so sweet and helpless," Kirsty said. "Even if she is a stranger."

Suddenly, a puff of fairy sparkles erupted from a nearby umbrella stand.

A tiny fairy popped her head up—it was Aisha the Princess and the Pea Fairy!

"She's not a stranger!" Aisha said. "I know who she is!"

The Lost Princess

Kirsty and Rachel smiled at Aisha. She wore a cute, dark pink top with a matching flowy skirt. She had long black braids that fell past her shoulders. Her tiny, pink heeled shoes were decorated with black pom-poms.

"Aisha!" Kirsty cried. "It's so nice to see you again."

Rachel looked at the young woman in the doorway. "If you're here, that means that she—"

"Is the princess from *The Princess and the Pea*," finished Aisha.

The young woman frowned. "Princess? Pea?" she asked. Then she sighed. "I don't know what's wrong with me. I'm so confused!"

"You should come inside," Kirsty said quickly.

Aisha fluttered up to the princess. "You've lost your memory . . . sort of," she explained. "But don't worry, I'll help you, and so will my friends Kirsty and Rachel."

The princess nodded. "Thank you," she said, and then she shivered. "It's cold in here."

"We should get her some dry clothes," Rachel said. "I'm sure we could find something in her size in the costume closet."

Kirsty nodded and looked at Aisha. "Do you want to fly into my pocket? We have to make sure nobody sees you."

"Of course!" Aisha replied with a smile, and she flew into the front pocket of Kirsty's sweater.

Rachel turned to the princess. "Follow us."

The girls led the princess through the big castle ballroom. Nobody noticed the rain-drenched princess with the girls. Everyone was too worried about the missing mattresses.

They walked down a hallway and then stopped in front of the costume closet. It was filled with costumes for the festival organizers and costumes for the children to borrow, too. Kirsty opened the door and they stepped inside. The big closet was filled with racks of dresses, fancy jackets and pants, furry animal suits, and scarves and jewelry in every color.

"What would you like to wear?" Rachel asked.

"It doesn't matter, as long as it's dry," the princess said. "Thank you. It's very kind of you."

Aisha fluttered out of Kirsty's pocket. "I see something," she said, alighting next to a dark pink princess dress. "It's the same color as mine!"

The princess pulled it off the hanger. "It's very pretty, and it looks like it will fit."

“You can change in our room,” Rachel offered.

They went back upstairs to the bedroom the girls shared.

“Our mattresses are still here,” Kirsty remarked, as they stepped inside.

“Why wouldn’t they be?” Aisha asked.

“Let’s step outside so the princess can get changed, and we’ll explain,” Rachel said.

Aisha and the girls left the room and closed the door. Aisha flew out of Kirsty’s pocket and sat on her shoulder.

"What were you saying about mattresses?" she asked.

"Somebody has been stealing all the mattresses in the castle," Rachel replied.

"And that made me think of The Princess and the Pea fairy tale," Kirsty said. "In the story, the queen makes the princess sleep on a big pile of mattresses."

"This is very interesting," Aisha said. "I came here looking for Jack Frost. He has my magic golden locket. Without it, I can't control The Princess and the Pea fairy tale. I know that Jack Frost wants to make himself the star of the story!"

"Do you think Jack Frost is the reason the mattresses are missing?" Rachel asked.

"It could be," Aisha said. "To be the star of *The Princess and the Pea*, he would need a lot of mattresses!"

Just then the door opened, and the princess stood there wearing the pink dress. She looked very different from the young woman who had knocked on the castle door.

"Oh, you look so much happier!" Rachel said.

"Thank you," the princess said with a smile. "Now, I just wish I knew why I was here. I think I'm supposed to be in a castle, but I'm not sure if this is the right one."

They all walked back inside the girls' room.

"You should stay here while we go try to figure this out," Aisha told the princess.

"I have some books you could read," Rachel offered.

"Thank you," the princess said.

"You're welcome—by the way, what is your name?" Rachel asked.

The princess frowned. "I don't know. I can't seem to remember."

Aisha flew between the girls. "In the fairy tale, the princess doesn't have a name," she said. "I just call her Princess."

"We'll be back soon, Princess," Kirsty promised. She turned to Rachel and Aisha. "We should start by looking for Jack Frost. He and his goblins could be—"

"Hey, quit poking me!" whined a scratchy voice.

The girls froze. "Did you hear that?" Rachel asked.

They heard more voices.

"Ow!"

"Knock it off!"

"Those voices are coming from under the bed!" Kirsty cried. She ran to her bed and lifted up the bedspread. Two green goblin faces scowled back at her.

"What are you doing here?" Kirsty demanded.

The two goblins scrambled out from their hiding place.

“We’re stealing your mattress!” one goblin replied.

The other goblin nudged him. “Don’t tell them that!”

“But it’s true!” said the other. “Anyway, Jack Frost asked us to steal it, so we have to. And don’t try to stop us!”

The two goblins grabbed the mattress.

“Oh, no you don’t!” Kirsty said.

“That’s right! You get out of here!” added Rachel.

The princess picked up her wet dress and waved it at them. “Get out of here! Shoo! Shoo!”

The goblins swatted away the dress and grabbed the mattress out before the girls could react!

"This is our mattress now," they cackled, and ran out of the room.

"Follow them!" Aisha cried. "They may lead us to Jack Frost!"

The Sweet Jack Frost?

The girls chased the goblins down the hallway. Aisha flew with them, her shimmering wings fluttering on her back.

At the end of the hall, the goblins turned right. As the girls followed them around the corner, they saw the goblins push open a door into one of the bedrooms.

"In there!" Kirsty yelled.

The girls stopped at the door and peeked inside. Aisha hovered above them.

Inside, Jack Frost was sitting at a dressing table. He held a big fluffy powder puff and was patting it against his long, pointy nose. A gold, heart-shaped locket hung around his neck from a gold chain.

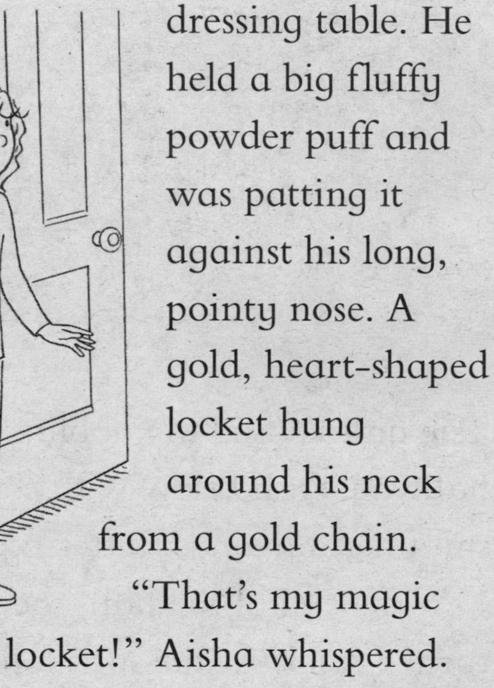

"That's my magic locket!" Aisha whispered.

"My skin is so delicate, soft, and sweet! Next I will powder my delicate feet!" Jack Frost was singing.

"Sweet? Delicate?" Kirsty whispered out loud. "Him?"

Jack Frost noticed the two goblins standing behind him.

"Why are you just standing there?" he snapped. "And why don't you have lots of more mattresses for me?"

"Well, we got this one, but . . ." one goblin started to explain.

"But what?" Jack Frost fumed. "I don't want to hear any excuses. I need lots of mattresses so I can be the star of The Princess and the Pea fairy tale!"

"It's just as we thought," Aisha whispered. "He wants to sleep on a tall stack of mattresses, just like the princess in the story."

"But where is he hiding them all?" Kirsty wondered.

Just then, two more goblins carrying a mattress pushed past Kirsty and Rachel to get into the room.

"Oh, good! This will just about do it!" Jack Frost said. "Now stand back."

The two goblins propped the mattress up against the wall and backed away from it. Jack Frost picked up his wand from the dresser and pointed it at the mattress.

Poof! The mattress disappeared.

"He's sending them back to his castle," Rachel guessed.

"Now all of you, go get me more mattresses," Jack Frost ordered. "I am busy getting my delicate skin nice and soft so that tonight, I will feel the pea under all of the mattresses. And when I do, the fairy tale will be known as *Jack Frost and the Pea*!"

Aisha gasped. "I must get that locket from him!"

"We'll distract him," Rachel said, and Kirsty nodded. Then the two girls ran into the room.

"Stop right there, Jack Frost!" Kirsty demanded.

"You!" Jack Frost cried. "Can't you just leave me alone?"

"No!" Rachel said. "You stole Aisha's

locket and now you're trying to steal a fairy tale. That's not very nice."

Jack Frost stood up. "Oh, but it *will* be very nice! Children around the world will read *Jack Frost and the Pea.* I'll be much better in the role than some silly princess."

Rachel and Kirsty watched Aisha fly behind Jack Frost so she could get the locket off his neck.

"Princesses aren't silly," Rachel argued. "You're the silly one if you think you can feel a pea under all of those mattresses."

"I will, once I am finished powdering my delicate skin," Jack Frost said. He patted the powder puff against his nose again. A cloud of powder filled the air. It hit Aisha's nose just as she was about to unlock the clasp.

"Achoo!" Aisha sneezed.

"What was that?" Jack Frost cried, spinning around. Then he saw Aisha. "Fairy!"

"Give me my locket, Jack Frost!" Aisha said. "It doesn't belong to you."

"Never!" Jack Frost cried. He clapped the puff against his hand, and another cloud of powder floated up. Aisha coughed and tumbled backward in the air.

Then Jack Frost pointed his wand at Rachel and Kirsty.

"I am tired of you two spoiling my plans!" he said. "I am going to *poof* you away from here so far that you will never get back. How do the icy plains of Antarctica sound?"

He aimed his wand at the girls, and a blast of icy magic came out. But before it could touch them . . .

Wham! The princess rushed into the room and tackled Rachel and Kirsty, knocking them out of the way of the magic blast. The blast hit the wall behind them.

“Rats!” Jack Frost cried. “I am tired of everyone ruining my fun! It’s time to go star in my fairy tale!”

Poof! He waved his wand once more and he and his goblins disappeared in a cloud of icy magic.

So Many Mattresses!

Rachel and Kirsty got to their feet. Aisha shook her wings to get the powder off.

"Sorry I knocked you down," the princess said.

"That's okay. You saved us!" said Rachel. "But how did you find us?"

"I saw two goblins walk past your room carrying a mattress," she replied.

"I thought that looked suspicious, so I followed them. Then I hung back to see what was happening."

"We're glad you did," Kirsty said. "So now what do we do?"

"We must follow Jack Frost to his castle," Aisha said, "and find some way to stop him before he changes the fairy tale forever. I will turn you girls into fairies so that you can go there."

"What about the princess?" Rachel asked.

"She can stay here if she wants, but she doesn't need to turn into a fairy to visit Fairyland," Aisha replied.

"Because she's from a fairy tale?" Kirsty guessed.

"Exactly!" Aisha said.

"I'd like to go with you," the princess

said. "You're doing a very nice thing by trying to help me. I'd like to help, too, if I can."

"Then let's go!" Aisha said. She waved her wand, and tiny hearts and peas spilled out in a glittery cloud. The girls shrunk to fairy-size and felt their gauzy wings fluttering on their backs.

Then Aisha waved her wand again, and there was a tinkling sound as she transported them all to Jack Frost's Ice Castle. Goblins marched back and forth across the castle entrance.

"The three of us can fly in," Aisha said. "Princess, I'm afraid you may have to wait out here."

The princess nodded. "Okay. I'll try to find a way past those goblins in the meantime."

Aisha, Kirsty, and Rachel flew up, up, up to the tall castle turrets. They found an open window and fluttered inside. Right away, they heard a commotion nearby.

"Hold it steady! I'm going to fall!" Jack Frost was yelling.

They flew into the main hall of Jack Frost's castle, where they saw an amazing sight.

Mattresses were stacked from the floor all the way up to the high ceiling, making a tall tower.

"One, two, three, four . . . there are too many to count!" Kirsty cried.

Jack Frost was trying to climb a long, rickety ladder all the way to the top. Two goblins stood below, steadying the ladder.

"The ladder is wiggling!" Jack Frost complained.

"Why don't you just use your wand to transport yourself up there?" one of the goblins called up.

"Because that's not in the fairy tale," Jack Frost called down. "I am a poor lost princess who needs a place to sleep for the night, and I'm going to climb up to the top of these mattresses, just like she did!"

Aisha and the girls watched as Jack Frost climbed and climbed until he

reached the top. Two goblins perched close to the edge, watching Jack Frost scramble to reach them.

"Pull me up!" Jack Frost demanded.

The goblins grabbed his hands and pulled Jack Frost onto the top mattress. The whole mattress tower wobbled dangerously.

"I have a plan," Aisha told the girls. "You two fly over and grab his wand. Then I'll try to get the locket."

"Got it!" Rachel and Kirsty said together, nodding.

The three fairies flew up to the top of the tower.

"I should be feeling the pea just about now," Jack was saying. "As I fall asleep, my delicate skin will feel the pea. Then everyone will know I am a true princess!"

"What pea?" asked one of the goblins.

"The pea that you put under the very bottom mattress," replied Jack Frost.

The goblins looked at one another.

Jack Frost sat straight up. "Do you mean to tell me you forgot to put the pea under the mattresses?" he wailed.

That's when he spotted the three fairies flying toward him. He quickly pointed at them.

"Goblins! Get rid of them!" he barked.

The goblins produced flyswatters and began

to swat at the fairies. Kirsty and Aisha quickly flew out of the way, but Rachel was just a little slower. One of the flyswatters hit her wings!

"Oh no!" Rachel cried, as she tumbled to the floor below.

Tumbling Down

"I'll help you!" Aisha cried. She started to wave her wand, but one of the goblins swatted it out of her hands.

"Oh no!" Aisha cried, and dove to catch it.

Kirsty flew as fast as she could. She had to reach Rachel before it was too late! But Rachel was almost near the bottom of the tower now.

"Rachel!" Kirsty cried out in alarm.

Rachel tried to flap her wings, but they wouldn't work!

"I've got you!" said a familiar voice.

Rachel landed safely in two soft hands. She looked up to see that the princess had caught her.

"Are you all right?" the princess asked.

"Just a little dizzy," Rachel said, standing up. "Thanks! You saved me again. But how did you get into the castle?"

Kirsty and Aisha flew up to them.

"Well, I hid and roared like a scary bear, and the goblins guarding the entrance ran away," the princess explained. "Then I ran inside. I guess I got here just in time."

Kirsty looked up at the top of the mattress tower. "If we go back up there, we'll just get swatted down again."

"I can't go back up there anyway," Rachel said. "My wings aren't working very well."

"As soon as I find my wand, I'll fix them," Aisha promised. She sighed. "I'm not quite sure what to do!"

Rachel looked up and down the mattresses. "If we can't go to Jack Frost, maybe we can bring him to us!"

"You mean knock down the mattress tower?" Kirsty asked. "Great idea! It's already so wobbly. It should fall over pretty easily."

She flew to one of the mattresses and pushed with all of her might. "They're too heavy! I wish I was my normal size. Then I'd be able to knock this whole tower right over!"

"Well, I'm my normal size," the princess said. "I can try."

Suddenly, two goblins ran up to them. One of them was holding Aisha's tiny wand!

"Jack Frost wants you out of here!" the goblin yelled.

Kirsty looked at the princess. "Aisha and I will get rid of the goblins," she whispered. "Once we're clear, you and Rachel can bring down the tower!"

The princess nodded. "Got it!"

"Catch us if you can!" Kirsty called out, and she and Aisha flew right past the goblins. They ran after the two fairies.

"All right, Rachel," the princess said. "I'm going to put you in the pocket of my dress. Then we'll both give a big push."

"Okay!" said Rachel, as the princess tucked her into the pocket.

The princess walked up to the mattress tower and began to push. Rachel pushed, too. The tower began to wobble even harder.

"What's happening?" Jack Frost yelled from high above.

"Almost there," the princess said. "One more push, Rachel!"

The princess and Rachel pushed with all their might. The tower teetered, and tottered, and then . . . all of the mattresses toppled over!

"I'm falling!" Jack Frost wailed.

One Clever Princess

Thump! Thump! Thump! The mattresses fell all over the floor of the castle's main hall. Jack Frost tumbled and rolled down the falling tower.

"Oof! Oof! Oof!" Jack Frost cried. "My poor delicate skin!"

As he somersaulted down the mattresses, Aisha's locket slipped off his neck and soared through the air.

"Got it!" Aisha yelled as she swooped across the room to grab it. The locket shrank to fairy-size in her hand.

Thump! Jack and the goblins landed safely on top of some soft mattresses.

“We did it!” Rachel cheered from the princess’s pocket. Then she looked around. “Where’s Kirsty?” She suddenly felt worried. What if Kirsty had been squished by a falling mattress?

“I’m here!” Kirsty said, flying over to everyone. “And I found Aisha’s wand!”

“Oh, thank you!” Aisha said. “Now I can fix Rachel’s wings.”

Aisha flew to Rachel and waved her wand. A musical sound filled the air as tiny hearts and peas swirled around Rachel’s wings. They began to flutter, and she flew out of the princess’s pocket.

"Hooray!" she cheered. Then she turned to the princess. "Thanks for all your help."

"It was fun," the princess said. Her body started to shimmer.

"What's happening?" Kirsty asked.

"Now that I have my magic locket back, she can return to her fairy tale," Aisha explained.

"I have something to say before I go!" the princess said. "I remember my fairy tale now. In the story, I feel the pea under the mattresses and prove that I'm a real princess. But that's not what really happened."

"It isn't?" the girls asked, surprised.

The princess shook her head. "Not exactly. You see, I thought it was strange that the queen asked me to sleep on so many mattresses. So I looked under them and found the pea. I guessed what the queen was up to and played along. Nobody could really feel a pea under all those mattresses! That would be silly."

"That's exactly what I said!" Kirsty cried.

The princess's body shimmered even more, and she waved as she faded away.

"And that is the mark of a true princess," Aisha said. "It's not delicate skin. It's cleverness!"

"And bravery," Rachel added. "She

saved me twice and wasn't afraid of Jack Frost or his goblins."

"Speaking of Jack Frost—he could use a little more cleverness right now," Kirsty said, nodding over to the center of the hall. Jack Frost and his goblins were trying to stand up in the pile of mattresses, but kept falling over. Their arms and legs flailed about wildly.

"Somebody help me!" Jack Frost cried.

"But I can't get up!" one of the goblins yelled.

Aisha smiled. "Let's get you girls back to Tiptop Castle before Jack Frost manages to get up and starts causing trouble."

She waved her wand again, and the girls instantly found themselves back in their room in Tiptop Castle. Their wings

were gone, and they were normal-size once again.

"Thank you both so much for all your help," Aisha said. "I'm going back to Jack Frost's castle so that I can send all the mattresses back here."

"Be careful!" Rachel said.

"I will," Aisha promised, and then she vanished.

As the last of Aisha's fairy magic twinkled away, the girls heard a commotion coming from downstairs.

"Let's go see what's happening," Rachel suggested.

They headed downstairs to find all of the festival organizers and guests in the ballroom. A big movie screen had been set up, and the chairs were organized in rows, like in a movie theater. The castle cooks were setting up at a table at the back of the room. They were handing out hot dogs and popcorn to the children.

The girls spotted Omri and another girl they had met, Emily.

"What's going on?" Rachel asked.

"We're going to watch a fairy tale movie!" Emily said. "You're just in time."

"You'd better hurry and get your hot dogs and popcorn," Omri said. "We'll save you a seat."

Rachel patted her stomach. "Thanks! I forgot how long ago breakfast was."

The girls grabbed their food and took seats next to Omri and Emily. The lights dimmed, and the movie started.

"Has there ever been a movie made about *The Princess and the Pea*?" Kirsty whispered to Rachel.

"I don't think so," Rachel replied. "But that would make a good movie, I think."

Kirsty nodded. "Yes, especially if the real princess was the star!"

After the film ended, the lights came on in the ballroom.

"It's still raining out," Amy reported. "There's a special craft set up in the dining room."

"That sounds like fun!" Emily said. She looked at Kirsty and Rachel. "Are you going to do it?"

The girls looked at each other. They were both thinking the same thing.

"We need to check something in our room first," Rachel said. "We'll be right back."

As the girls made their way to their room, they heard surprised voices coming from some of the other rooms.

"My mattress is back!"

"So is mine!"

"Somebody returned all the mattresses!"

Kirsty grinned. "I guess Aisha didn't have any trouble back at Jack Frost's castle."

When they got to their room, Rachel picked up *The Fairies' Book of Fairy Tales* and flipped through it.

"It's here!" she cried. "*The Princess and the Pea*. The fairy tale is safe from Jack Frost."

"We still have to save *The Little Mermaid*," Kirsty said. "Can you imagine Jack Frost as a mermaid?"

Rachel shook her head. "Jack Frost with a long fish tail? No way!"

"Well, if he comes back to Tiptop Castle I'm sure we'll find a way to get the last magic object back to Fairy Tale Lane," Kirsty said.

"We'll do it princess-style," Rachel said.

Kirsty grinned. "With cleverness!"

"And bravery!" Rachel added.

THE FAIRY TALE FAIRIES

Rachel and Kirsty found Julia's, Eleanor's, Faith's, Rita's, Gwen's, and Aisha's missing magic objects. Now it's time for them to help

Lacey
the Little Mermaid Fairy!

Join their next adventure in this special sneak peek . . .

Kirsty and Rachel recognized Lacey the Little Mermaid Fairy right away—she was just as sparkly as they remembered! Lacey's delicate wings glistened in the sunshine and her mermaid tail sparkled with pale purple scales. Her dark hair was held in place with a fine golden headband. Along the bottom of her shirt a row of tiny jewels glinted in the light.

"We're always ready to help a fairy," whispered Rachel, kneeling over the side of the fountain to make sure that no one else would see Lacey.

"Always," echoed Kirsty. "What can we do?"

Lacey's pretty smile faded. "It's my fairy tale." She sighed. "I can't go on for a minute longer without putting things right!"

"Is there still no sign of your magic object?" wondered Rachel.

Lacey shook her head sadly.

"What does it look like?" asked Kirsty.

"It's an oyster shell with a pearl inside," replied Lacey. "It's very precious.

The characters from *The Little Mermaid* have been gone for days now. The shell could be anywhere!"

"We'll find it somehow," promised Rachel.

"There must be somewhere new that we can search," said Kirsty. "Let's think . . ."

"Hey! Over here!"

Lacey and the girls looked up. Someone was shouting from the other side of the courtyard. Another voice bellowed a reply:

"Look at that!"

"It's splashing all over the place!" yelled a third voice.

"Don't just stare at it—let's get it!" boomed another.

Lacey flipped out of the water. "That

noise," she cried breathlessly. "It's coming from the moat."

"We need to get there fast!" urged Rachel.

Kirsty began to run, but Lacey shook her head.

"You'll be faster as fairies," she said, pointing her wand into the fountain. As soon as the wand touched the water, a wave of miniature golden shells showered in all directions. Lacey beckoned for the girls to put their hands underneath it. Kirsty and Rachel gazed in wonder as the shells tickled and popped on their fingers before disappearing into the spray. Soon the girls were covered in a sparkling mist of gold.

"We're getting smaller!" exclaimed Kirsty.

When the mist cleared, Rachel reached up to touch her shoulders. A gauzy pair of fairy wings had appeared. The friends joined hands, then fluttered into the air.

"Hey, you!" shouted the voices again. "Come here!"

Kirsty, Rachel, and Lacey hurried across the courtyard, following the noisy shouts. They flew out past the gatehouse, across the drawbridge, and over the moat.

"Oh my!" cried Lacey, nearly tumbling out of the sky. "Goblins!"

Kirsty and Rachel looked down. Floating on the moat, in among the lily pads, was an inflatable raft. Four green goblins were sitting on it, fighting over a giant fishing net.

"She's too heavy!" moaned one goblin, tugging the net with all his might.

"Let me have a try," barked another, shoving his friend out of the way. The goblin heaved and hauled the net until—*plop!*—it landed on the raft. The rest of the gang hooted in delight. A mermaid suddenly popped her head out of the net, then sat up in the middle of the raft.

Lacey gasped. "It's the Little Mermaid from my fairy tale!"

RAINBOW magic™

Which Magical Fairies Have You Met?

- ❑ The Rainbow Fairies
- ❑ The Weather Fairies
- ❑ The Jewel Fairies
- ❑ The Pet Fairies
- ❑ The Dance Fairies
- ❑ The Music Fairies
- ❑ The Sports Fairies
- ❑ The Party Fairies
- ❑ The Ocean Fairies
- ❑ The Night Fairies
- ❑ The Magical Animal Fairies
- ❑ The Princess Fairies
- ❑ The Superstar Fairies
- ❑ The Fashion Fairies
- ❑ The Sugar & Spice Fairies
- ❑ The Earth Fairies
- ❑ The Magical Crafts Fairies
- ❑ The Baby Animal Rescue Fairies
- ❑ The Fairy Tale Fairies

SCHOLASTIC

Find all of your favorite fairy friends at
scholastic.com/rainbowmagic

RMFAIRY13

RAINBOW magic™

Magical fun for everyone!
Learn fairy secrets, send friendship notes, and more!

SCHOLASTIC

www.scholastic.com/rainbowmagic

RMACTIV4

SPECIAL EDITION

Which Magical Fairies Have You Met?

- ❑ Joy the Summer Vacation Fairy
- ❑ Holly the Christmas Fairy
- ❑ Kylie the Carnival Fairy
- ❑ Stella the Star Fairy
- ❑ Shannon the Ocean Fairy
- ❑ Trixie the Halloween Fairy
- ❑ Gabriella the Snow Kingdom Fairy
- ❑ Juliet the Valentine Fairy
- ❑ Mia the Bridesmaid Fairy
- ❑ Flora the Dress-Up Fairy
- ❑ Paige the Christmas Play Fairy
- ❑ Emma the Easter Fairy
- ❑ Cara the Camp Fairy
- ❑ Destiny the Rock Star Fairy
- ❑ Belle the Birthday Fairy
- ❑ Olympia the Games Fairy
- ❑ Selena the Sleepover Fairy
- ❑ Cheryl the Christmas Tree Fairy
- ❑ Florence the Friendship Fairy
- ❑ Lindsay the Luck Fairy
- ❑ Brianna the Tooth Fairy
- ❑ Autumn the Falling Leaves Fairy
- ❑ Keira the Movie Star Fairy
- ❑ Addison the April Fool's Day Fairy
- ❑ Bailey the Babysitter Fairy
- ❑ Natalie the Christmas Stocking Fairy
- ❑ Lila and Myla the Twins Fairies
- ❑ Chelsea the Congratulations Fairy
- ❑ Carly the School Fairy
- ❑ Angelica the Angel Fairy
- ❑ Blossom the Flower Girl Fairy

SCHOLASTIC

Find all of your favorite fairy friends at
scholastic.com/rainbowmagic

RMSPECIAL17